Jennifer
the Babysitter
Fairy

Special thanks to
Mandy Archer

ORCHARD BOOKS
338 Euston Road, London NW1 3BH
Orchard Books Australia
Level 17/207 Kent Street, Sydney, NSW 2000
A Paperback Original

First published in 2013 by Orchard Books

HiT entertainment

A CIP catalogue record for this book is available
from the British Library.

ISBN 978 1 40832 510 0

1 3 5 7 9 10 8 6 4 2

Printed in Great Britain

The paper and board used in this paperback are natural recyclable
products made from wood grown in sustainable forests. The
manufacturing processes conform to the environmental regulations
of the country of origin.

Orchard Books is a division of Hachette Children's Books,
an Hachette UK company

www.hachette.co.uk

Jennifer
the Babysitter
Fairy

by Daisy Meadows

ORCHARD

www.rainbowmagic.co.uk

The Fairyland Palace

Fairyland Nursery

Eco Lodges

EcoWorld

Kirsty and
Rachel's lodge

Treetop
Café

Jack Frost's Spell

Goblins botch and goblins fumble,
Goblins shout and goblins grumble,
Got to fix this naughty rabble,
Poked-out tongues and noisy gabble.

All babysitters best beware,
I'll snatch the objects in your care,
Precious things from precious tots,
As they lie curled up in their cots.

Toy Box
Trouble

Contents

The Holiday Begins!

"Rachel, look!" gasped Kirsty Tate, peeping out of the lodge window. "We can see the butterfly house from our bedroom!"

Rachel Walker dropped her suitcase and ran round to the other side of the bed. As soon as she drew back the jolly polka-dot print curtain, her face lit up with a smile.

"I can see it!" she replied. There, almost hidden among the trees, was a cluster of cabins and glasshouses in all different shapes and sizes. The butterfly house was the one in the middle, next to the main eco-centre. Inside, tropical plants and blossoms curled up towards the sunshine, filling the dome with rainbow colours.

It was the perfect beginning to the girls' spring break. Kirsty and Rachel had only just arrived, but they loved it here already! Their families had organised this weekend away at the EcoWorld activity centre – an amazing park set in the heart of a leafy forest. Mr and Mrs Tate's friends, the Robinsons, had been invited too.

Everything at EcoWorld had been carefully designed to protect the animals and plants that lived in the countryside around it. The Tates, Walkers and Robinsons were spending the weekend in a pretty eco-lodge built out of reclaimed wood. Everything in the park was recycled, even the water in the swimming pools!

Kirsty picked up her EcoWorld

brochure and started flicking through the pages.

"Shall we go exploring?" she said. "It says there's a climbing wall here and a rainforest area and…wow! Rachel, the dome with the man-made lake has a roof that opens up when its sunny!"

Rachel couldn't help but giggle – she'd grabbed her fleece already! She and Kirsty had three precious days together and she wanted to make the most of every minute.

"I wonder what we'll find today?" she mused.

Kirsty's eyes twinkled. She and Rachel were used to discovering all sorts of amazing, magical things. The lucky girls shared a secret – they were friends with the fairies! The pair had been on some incredible adventures. Jack Frost and his goblin servants were always stomping into Fairyland and trying to stir up trouble. If a fairy needed their help, they only had to wave their magic wand and Rachel and Kirsty would be there.

The girls slipped on their fleeces and scampered out into the garden.

The lodge had large glass doors that opened onto a daisy-speckled lawn.

"Kirsty! Kirsty!" chimed a little voice.

"Play! Play!" piped up another.

Kirsty and Rachel beamed at each other. The friends swished aside the branches of a pretty weeping willow and spotted Tom and Lily, Mr and Mrs Robinson's two-year-old twins. The toddlers were playing in a sandpit made out of recycled railway sleepers.

"Hello, you two!" exclaimed Kirsty. "This is my best friend, Rachel."

"Ra-ra," cooed Lily.

Rachel bent down to meet the excited twins. Lily played peekaboo behind her hands, but Tom gave her a wide, cheeky smile.

Tom glanced at Lily, then shyly presented their new friend with a shiny orange spade.

"We can't play right now, Tom," Kirsty said kindly, "but we'll come back and build sandcastles later."

Rachel nodded. "We just want to see what there is to do in EcoWorld."

The adorable little boy clapped his
hands. He'd spotted Mrs Tate wandering
up to the sandpit with his drink bottle.
Kirsty's mum pulled a crumpled list and
some money out of her jeans pocket.

"Would you pick me up a few bits
from the supermarket?" she asked.
"Just follow the boardwalks, the park
is totally enclosed. Use the change to
treat yourselves to a shake at the café
afterwards if you like."

"Great!" grinned
Kirsty.

She linked arms
with Rachel,
steering her
towards a path at
the bottom of the
garden.

"Isn't this brilliant?" remarked Rachel, as the friends stepped onto a maze of boardwalks. Every so often, the walkway would turn a corner to reveal a building nestled in the canopy of trees.

The friends rushed to the supermarket and picked out Mrs Tate's groceries. Soon they were sitting in the Treetop Café, each clutching a tasty milkshake.

"I'll get some straws," offered Kirsty, spotting a container in the corner.

She lifted the lid and picked out two straws with glittering stripes. She took them back to the table.

Rachel blinked, then peered around the café. Was she imagining it, or did her straw seem to be sparkling more brightly than everyone else's?

A Fairy Friend in Need

The sparkly straw was shimmering brilliantly now. Kirsty had never seen a straw twinkle before – it had to be fairy magic! Rachel propped the straw against her milkshake so that no one else in the café could see it.

"Thank you!" trilled a sweet singsong voice. "I've been waiting for you to arrive."

A tiny fairy stepped out from behind the milkshake glass. She was beautifully turned out in denim shorts, cropped leggings and a red scarf dotted with yellow spots. Her blonde hair swished as she moved, setting her freckles off to perfection.

"My name's Jennifer the Babysitter Fairy," she said, waving a tiny hand. "I work in the Fairyland Nursery."

"We're so pleased to meet you!" gasped Kirsty. "I'm Kirsty, by the way, and this is Rachel."

Jennifer nodded her head, but her smile seemed sad.

"I know all about you both," she replied, "*and* everything that you've done for the fairies. That's why I came here today."

"Is something wrong?' Rachel asked quietly.

Jennifer's eyes filled up with tears. Something was very wrong indeed!

"It's my job to look after the fairy babies," she explained, before adding, "Not on my own, of course. All of the fairies take turns to help in the Fairyland Nursery. The Sporty Fairies are always popping in to play games and the Rainbow Fairies love sharing their painting spells."

"That sounds wonderful," said Kirsty.

"It is," replied Jennifer. "Or at least it *was*…until Jack Frost stole my three magical objects!"

"The rainforest zone is next door," suggested Rachel. "Let's find a quiet place and talk properly."

Kirsty agreed. She helped Jennifer climb into the shopping bag so they could smuggle her outside. The girls slipped out of the café and tiptoed into the damp, warm air of the rainforest dome. The huge glass pod was alive with jungle plants – from towering trees to stunning tropical flowers. Every few moments the lightest shower of rain would sprinkle down from special hoses in the ceiling.

"Over here," said Rachel, pointing towards a little glade hidden by giant palms.

When they were sure that the coast was clear, Jennifer peeped out of the shopping bag. She fluttered like a butterfly in a circle around the girls, her golden wings lighting up the shadows.

"Fairyland is in the most terrible trouble," she said urgently. She settled next to a puddle of rainwater, then touched it with her wand. The puddle began to swirl and mist over.

Kirsty nudged Rachel — Jennifer was creating a magical Seeing Pool! The water cleared, revealing a cheerful playroom decorated with colourful pictures and twinkly lights. Along one end were ten tiny cots, each covered with a chiffon canopy trimmed with the finest fairy embroidery.

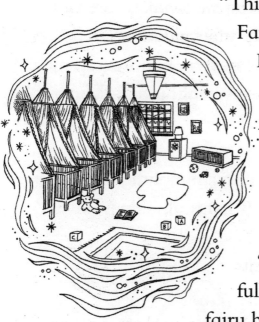

"This is the
Fairyland
Nursery,"
sighed
Jennifer,
peering
sorrowfully
into the
water.
"Usually it's
full of happy
fairy babies."

Rachel's heart leapt. In all of their
adventures together, the girls had *never*
met any fairy babies!

"What are those?" asked Kirsty,
pointing to three quilted cushions.

"That's where I keep my precious
objects!" replied the Babysitter Fairy.

"The magical toy box makes sure that everyone enjoys their playtimes. The magical snack pack enchants every meal so that food tastes healthy and delicious."

"And the third one?" Rachel wondered out loud.

"That's the magical nightlight," said Jennifer. "It helps all babies have restful naps and sweet dreams at bedtime. The poor little dears will be worn out without it!"

The troubled fairy began to shed silvery tears. As they dropped into the water, each one made the tiniest tinkling sound.

"Please don't cry," said Kirsty. "Between the three of us, we'll get your magical objects back. Won't we, Rachel?"

Rachel nodded her head as hard as she could.

"Of course we will!" she agreed. "When did they disappear?"

"This afternoon," Jennifer answered, "in the middle of storytime."

Suddenly the rainforest water began to shine like a mirror. The girls saw the Fairyland Nursery again, but now it was full of adorable fairy babies.

The little ones were sitting in a circle, gurgling happily. Jennifer was reading a fairy story, conjuring up floating pictures with her wand.

"Look!" gasped Kirsty, pointing to the back of the playroom.

Three ugly goblins were climbing in through the window, each disguised as a giant baby! The silly threesome pretended to crawl across a rug, mumbling daft baby noises under their breath.

"Goo goo, ga ga!" babbled one, hitching up a badly wrapped nappy.

"Babies are yucky," grumbled his mate. "This is the rottenest thing Jack Frost's ever made us do!"

"Be quiet!" snapped the third. "Just grab the gear and go!"

Kids' Club Chaos

Kirsty looked up from the pool and frowned. "So the goblins stole the three magical objects and took them back to Jack Frost's Ice Castle?" she asked, sadly.

Jennifer's wings drooped a little lower. "No," she exclaimed. "They decided to cause some mischief first! The goblins thought it would be very funny to hide the objects from us fairies. My precious things could be anywhere by now."

Rachel gulped.
Without the
magical toy
box, snack
pack and
nightlight,
children in
both the fairy
and human worlds wouldn't be very
happy at all.

"Let's start looking straight away," she
declared. "Babies need sleep, good food
and playtimes. We can't let Jack Frost
and his servants spoil those!"

"I knew you'd be able to help!"
beamed Jennifer. "I'll go back to
Fairyland and search for clues there.
I need to check on the nursery, too. The
Party Fairies are looking after the babies

this afternoon – the
babies love it
when Melodie
the Music
Fairy sings
for them!"

Jennifer
disappeared
in a shimmer
of scarlet
fairy dust.

Kirsty and
Rachel rushed back
to their lodge, running down the forest
paths as fast as their legs would carry
them. Both were wondering the same
thing – why would Jack Frost steal a
babysitter fairy's enchanted objects? It
made no sense at all.

"Lily! Tom! What's got into you today?"

As they slipped through the garden gate, Kirsty and Rachel could only just make out Mrs Robinson's voice – her words were being drowned out by the most terrible screeching! The twins were sitting in the middle of the lawn, thumping their little fists.

"That's not like them," whispered Kirsty, "and what happened to all the toys?"

Rachel's mouth dropped open. The garden was in a dreadful mess! The rakes and spades in the sandpit had been snapped in half, the trampoline had a hole in it and the twins' football had deflated. Tom and Lily's parents were crouching down next to the toddlers,

36

desperately trying to calm them down.

"I don't know how it happened." Mr
Robinson shrugged. "Every toy they
touched just fell apart!"

The girls shared a secret glance. They
both had a very good idea what was
going on! Until Jennifer's magical toy
box was back where it belonged, no one
would be able to enjoy playtime.

"Why don't we take the twins to the
kids' club for a couple of hours?" Rachel
suggested, handing over the shopping.

"Then you'll have a chance to get things straight again."

Mrs Robinson nodded her head gratefully.

"Thank you, girls," agreed Mr Robinson. "I think that will do us *all* good."

Rachel took Lily's hand and led her out towards the trail at the bottom of the garden. Kirsty followed behind with Tom. With two grouchy toddlers in tow, it took longer to get to the centre of the park than last time.

"Here we are!" announced Kirsty, finally spotting the "Sunnydays Kids' Club" sign.

The girls led the twins into a colourful reception area. Once Tom and Lily had been signed in, a playworker called

Diane came out to greet them.

"The toddlers are playing outside," she said wearily, showing her guests out to a walled garden decorated with cheery murals of ladybirds and bumblebees.

The garden was filled with children, but no one seemed to be having fun. The art and craft area on the patio was covered with toppled easels and snapped paintbrushes. On the lawn, a group of children were squabbling over a pot of bubbles.

"Yuck!" cried Lily, as a bubble popped on her jumper, covering her outfit in a horrible, sticky goo.

"Oh dear," sighed Diane. "The children are rather boisterous today."

Kirsty noticed a little boy snatching his friend's trike. In another corner of the garden, two girls were fighting over a teddy bear.

"Would you like us to give you a hand?" she offered. "It must be hard looking after all these children on your own."

"I would love some help," replied Diane, "but I'm not on my own. I've got a new nursery assistant on garden duty, but he doesn't seem to be very focused."

Diane pointed to the waterplay area. There, in the middle of the mayhem, was a figure standing in one of the troughs! Instead of calming down the toddlers, he was kicking water all over the ground.

Kirsty narrowed her eyes. She couldn't help but notice the stranger's large, crooked nose.

"Rachel!" she whispered. "We've found our first goblin!"

The Goblin Babysitter

As soon as Diane had led the twins off to find aprons, Rachel and Kirsty crept up for a closer look.

"That's a goblin all right!" whispered Rachel, ducking down behind a climbing frame.

The cheeky fellow had a baseball cap pulled down low and an apron tied round his middle, but his big green feet were a dead giveaway! Instead of having fun in the water, the goblin was muttering furiously under his breath.

"Pesky children!" he hissed. "I turn my back for one minute and they run off with the stupid toy box. Now my toes have gone soggy!"

Kirsty winked at her best friend – Jennifer's precious object had to be nearby!

"Where is it?" Kirsty wondered. "We have to get to the magical toy box before the goblin does."

As the girls were thinking, a soft breeze blew through their hair and tickled their cheeks. Sunbeams began to dance in the air, glinting brighter and brighter until – *pop!* – Jennifer the Babysitter Fairy appeared!

"Is there any news?" she asked anxiously, perching on the edge of the climbing frame.

Kirsty and Rachel told the little fairy all about the naughty goblin.

"Good work!" she chirped, her face flushing with relief. "I just knew that the magical toy box wasn't too far away."

Jennifer couldn't resist taking to the skies for an impromptu loop-the-loop, her golden wings glinting in the afternoon sun.

"We still need to find it," Rachel reminded her in a low voice. She pointed over to the water troughs – the sight of the noisy goblin was enough to get poor Jennifer in a flutter again.

"Let's start looking," she cried. "The magical toy box has a yellow lid and

46

pink panels on the sides."

"We'll have a better chance if we split up," suggested Kirsty. "Shall I start out here?"

The friends agreed. Jennifer flew up to the very top of the climbing frame so she could peep across the garden, while Rachel tiptoed inside.

The nursery was certainly quieter than the garden, but the children were just as unsettled. In the cosy corner, a flustered assistant was trying to read a fairy story to a group of unruly toddlers.

"Please *try* and listen," she begged. "Otherwise you won't find out what happened to Cinderella when the clock struck twelve."

"Don't care!" snapped a little boy, poking out his tongue.

The assistant turned the page over and did her best to carry on.

"'And then the wicked witch appeared...'" she read, before blurting out, "Wicked witch? There is no wicked witch in *Cinderella*!"

As the assistant grappled with the muddled pages, Rachel began to search through the toys at the back of the room. Kirsty soon joined her.

"Let's start over here," Rachel whispered, pulling out a drawer marked FARM ANIMALS. "Oh!"

Instead of farm animals, the drawer was crammed to bursting with mixed-up pieces of jigsaw puzzle. The next one down was labelled DINOSAURS, but there were only broken toy cars inside, gummed together with play dough.

"Where can it be?" sighed Rachel. "This can't go on!"

On the cushions, the toddlers had started to wail. One frustrated little girl even threw her fleecy blanket across the carpet! Rachel ran over to pick it up, stooping down next to a wooden play kitchen.

"Here you go," she smiled, handing the blanket back.

The little girl didn't look up. She was too busy peering at something sparkly inside the kitchen's oven.

"Oh my!" gasped Rachel, rushing out
to fetch her friends. "I think we've found
the magical toy box!"

As soon as Jennifer appeared, the girls
dashed over to the kitchen.

"Open the door," urged the Babysitter
Fairy. "Please hurry."

Rachel reached out for the oven, but a
knobbly, green hand bumped her out of
the way.

"Only Sunnydays workers allowed in
the role-play area," grunted the goblin.
"Hands off!"

Toddlers to the Rescue!

The goblin threw his head back and guffawed.

"Ha ha!" he roared. "You girls can't outsmart me! I'm the cleverest worker in this whole kids' club!"

Kirsty glanced around the playroom. Luckily the poor assistant was busy trying to tape the pages of her storybook back in the right order.

"Jennifer," she whispered quietly. "Would you like to hide behind me?"

"Yes, please!" gasped the nervous little fairy, darting into the strands of Kirsty's ponytail.

Rachel stepped forward to plead with the goblin, but the silly creature didn't give a hoot about the trouble he'd caused.

"Serves the kids right for being so horrible!" he crowed, blowing a big raspberry. "Human children give me the creeps. And babies! Babies are the worst!"

The goblin was so tickled with himself he did a jig on the spot, kicking his feet in crazy directions.

"Look! Look!"

The toddlers in the cosy corner had stopped crying. One by one they sat up and stared at the goblin's dance. The children began to clap their hands and point at the funny stranger.

"You are right," said Rachel, with a twinkle in her eye. "You really *are* the cleverest playworker. Look at all the children!"

"Eh?' asked the goblin, spinning on his heel.

The toddlers had formed a circle round Jack Frost's servant, their chubby cheeks pink with giggles. A little girl tugged at his apron and tried to hold his hand. Another boy tried to copy the goblin's dance, stamping his feet and wiggling his nappy.

"Help!" cried the imposter, shuddering
at the sight of so many thrilled faces.
"I'm under attack!"

The goblin shot into the air, but the
children just laughed
even harder. From her
secret hiding spot,
Jennifer couldn't help
giggling too.

"Goblins are
utterly terrified of
little ones," she trilled.
"How silly!"

The goblin couldn't bear it a moment
longer. Rachel and Kirsty watched the
daft creature stumble outside, waving
his arms in terror. The children thought
it was the best game ever, toddling after
him as fast as they could.

"Well, that's something I've never seen before," remarked Kirsty. "He's the goblin Pied Piper!"

The last thing the friends saw of the new assistant was a shaky figure clambering over the garden wall.

"I think Diane's new recruit has just resigned," said Rachel, opening the play kitchen's oven door. Inside was a glittering toy box with a brilliant yellow lid and bright pink sides.

"That's it!" cried Jennifer.
"That's my magical toy box!"
The delighted fairy
fluttered out into the open
in a flurry of twinkling stars.
She touched the edge of the toy
box with her wand and it swooshed
into her arms. Jennifer hugged the
precious object to her, then blew each of
the girls a heartfelt thank-you kiss.

"Now the children can play nicely
again," said Rachel.

Kirsty smiled happily. "You'd better
whisk the toy box to Fairyland, back
where it belongs!"

Jennifer agreed, but she had an
important job to do first. She thought for
a moment, then pointed her wand up to
the ceiling.

"Pitter patter, tiny feet,
Everything be smart and neat!"
There was a flash of gold light so
dazzling, Kirsty and Rachel had to close
their eyes. When they opened them
again, the nursery had been transformed!
All of the toys had been put back in
their places and there wasn't a broken
plaything in sight. The nursery assistant
was singing to herself as she put a
perfect copy of *Cinderella* back on the
bookshelf.

Outside it was just the same. The
garden looked immaculate! The children
were pottering happily on the lawn,
sharing their toys beautifully.

"Goodbye, girls," smiled Jennifer,
tucking the magical toy box under her
arm. "Thank you!"

60

"See you soon!" exclaimed Kirsty.

"And don't worry," added Rachel. "We'll keep an eye out for the other two magical items."

The best friends shared a secret smile, then ran over to find Tom and Lily.

"Now!" laughed Kirsty, scooping the twins up in a big hug. "Let's go back to the lodge and build some sandcastles!"

Picnics
in Peril

Contents

A Brand- New Day

"Morning, Kirsty!" said Rachel, throwing back her bedcovers.

"Morning!" exclaimed Kirsty. "Did you sleep well?"

Rachel nodded happily. Although her bed was comfy and soft, she had already been awake for ages. She couldn't wait to find out what the day had in store!

It was the girls' first morning waking up at EcoWorld and sunshine streamed in through the window. Kirsty stretched on her tiptoes. She could already hear the clinking of cereal bowls and the *ker-chink* of bread popping out of the toaster in the kitchen next door.

"Do you think we'll see Jennifer today?" asked Rachel, pulling on denim shorts and a purple T-shirt.

"I hope so!" replied Kirsty. "Jack Frost's goblins still have two of her magical objects."

Rachel frowned.

Until the magical snack pack and nightlight were back where they belonged in the Fairyland Nursery, poor Jennifer would have a tricky time looking after the fairy babies in her care.

As the friends combed their hair and brushed their teeth, they couldn't help wondering where the objects might be. It was tempting to run up and down the EcoWorld park prodding every bush and peering into every corner, but they knew that wouldn't do. Queen Titania had once told Kirsty and Rachel that they should always let fairy magic come to them. She'd also given both girls a precious golden locket filled with magical fairy dust. Just the merest sprinkle would turn them into fairies whenever their help was needed.

"Let's get some cornflakes," suggested Rachel. "Lily and Tom should be up by now."

The girls bounded into the kitchen to find both twins fastened into their highchairs.

"Kirsty!" squealed Tom, kicking his legs in delight.

Lily's rosy cheeks creased into happy dimples as she cooed, "Ra-ra!"

"She's trying to say my name!" said Rachel, clapping her hands. "Well done, Lily!"

Mrs Robinson wiped some mashed banana out of the scoop of Lily's bib.

"I wish the twins were as good at eating up their breakfast," she sighed. "They usually love banana, but they're more interested in throwing it across the room today."

Kirsty and Rachel poured themselves a bowl of cereal each. They sat down at the breakfast table, opposite the twins. Maybe if Tom and Lily saw *them* eating nicely the toddlers might be tempted to do the same!

"What would you like to do today, girls?" asked Mr Walker, using his cup of coffee to hold down the edge of a foldout map. He picked up his coffee cup and pushed the map across the table for the girls to look at.

71

"There's kayaking, mountain biking and archery," grinned Mr Tate. "I fancy having a go at the sailing!"

"Me too," Mrs Tate chipped in brightly. "The beginners' lesson starts at midday."

"The lake looks stunning," added Mr Robinson. "Kelly and I are up for sailing, aren't we, love?"

Mrs Robinson seemed keen, until she remembered that she'd booked the family onto a rainforest walk at the same time.

"It's being run by the Sunnydays Kids' Club," she explained. "There's going to be a trail to follow and a picnic in the centre of the dome. Tom and Lily would love it..."

Rachel and Kirsty exchanged excited glances. They'd both had exactly the same idea!

"Why don't we take the twins on the walk?" suggested Kirsty. "You can join us after your sailing lesson."

"They'd be more than happy with us," piped up Rachel, giving Lily a cheeky wink.

Mr and Mrs Robinson smiled gratefully at the girls – it was too good an offer to refuse!

The next hour was spent buzzing round the eco-lodge, tying shoes and filling up backpacks. Kirsty rummaged through a wooden chest and pulled out an extra picnic rug.

74

"Let's give it a shake in the garden," she suggested to Rachel.

The girls skipped outside, laughing as the blanket swished and flapped in the fresh air. As it unfurled, the leaves on the weeping willow at the bottom of the garden seemed to sing along with the gentle morning breeze.

"Look!" gasped Rachel, blinking in surprise.

A tiny fairy had tumbled out of the bottom of the picnic rug! Jennifer shook her golden hair, waved her wand then darted into the air.

"Hello!" she called. "I came as soon as I heard about the children's picnic. It's more important than ever that we find the magical snack pack!"

"You can count on us," replied Kirsty. "We'll be on the lookout."

Jennifer's eyes brightened. "Thank you, girls! I'll flutter back to Fairyland and keep watch there. We're having a picnic for the fairy babies today, too..."

Before Jennifer could say another word, footsteps pattered along the walkway at the bottom of the garden. Rachel clutched Kirsty's arm. The first children were making their way to the rainforest zone!

"If we want to stop the goblins from causing trouble," she warned, "we ought to go now!"

Trails and Tracks

"There you are, girls! The twins are all ready."

Jennifer had only just disappeared when Mrs Robinson pushed the double buggy out onto the patio. Tom and Lily both waved, their little faces rosy with excitement.

"'Phew!" whispered Kirsty, giving Rachel a secret nudge. "That was close!"

The tiniest trace of scarlet fairy dust still shimmered in the air around them, but Mrs Robinson didn't seem to notice. She was busy loading the buggy up with spare jumpers, wipes and teddies.

"I won't be long," she promised, flashing Kirsty and Rachel a grateful smile.

"There's no rush," replied Kirsty. "Enjoy the sailing!"

Rachel crouched down to grin at each of the twins, before adding, "We're going to have our own adventure, aren't we?"

"Yes, Ra-ra!" piped up Tom and Lily.

As soon as Mrs Robinson had kissed the toddlers goodbye, the friends unlatched the garden gate and wheeled the double buggy out onto the forest trail. The wooden walkway twisted in and out of the trees, curving past eco-lodges and leafy camping spots. Soon the rainforest dome appeared, creepers and vines curling up inside its glass windows.

The dome entrance was bustling with people. Babies peeped out of papooses, toddlers played tag around their mums' legs and grandparents took snaps with their cameras. A playworker stood at the doorway dressed in a Sunnydays Kids' Club T-shirt with a big smiley face printed on the front.

"There's Diane," said Kirsty.

"She seems much happier now that rotten old goblin has gone," added Rachel.

"Hello, Lily. Hello, Tom," said Diane, ticking their names off her list. "We're nearly ready to start our walk!"

Kirsty and Rachel parked the buggy and unfastened the twins. Diane held up her special Sunnydays flag, and everybody gathered round.

"Welcome to our wonderful rainforest," she announced. "You're free to explore the whole dome. The routes are full of animals, insects and flowers."

"Make sure you stay close," said Kirsty, reaching for the twins' hands.

"Good advice," praised Diane. "The dome is enormous – in fact it's a whole mini ecosystem! Luckily, every path leads to the waterfall in the centre. That's where we're going to have our Sunnydays picnic."

"Utterby! Utterby!" cooed Lily, tugging at Kirsty's hand. A butterfly with shimmering turquoise wings fluttered over the children's heads.

"OK," Kirsty chuckled. "We'll follow the 'utterby'!"

Diane handed Rachel a sketchbook and a packet of coloured pencils. There were five fun things for the twins to spot in the dome – a frog, a seed, a feather, a petal and a butterfly.

"I wonder if Tom and Lily can draw a picture of all five?" Diane asked with a smile.

At that moment, the turquoise butterfly settled on the end of the playworker's clipboard. The twins squealed with delight. They'd found one thing on the list already! Soon the pair were scampering up and down the rainforest paths, peeping through ferns and picking up pebbles.

"Look! Frog!" cried Tom, a few minutes later.

A tiny frog sat on the tip of a palm leaf, no bigger than a fairy. It looked up at the little boy and blinked.

"Isn't it sweet?" exclaimed Rachel, drawing a froggy shape for Lily to colour in.

"I've found something here, too," cried Kirsty.

"Is it the seed?" asked Rachel. "Or maybe the feather?"

Kirsty shook her head. There, set into

the soil, was the outline of an enormous, webbed foot. Only one creature that she could think of would leave a mark like that.

"Oh, Rachel," she gasped. "It's got to be a goblin footprint!"

Picnic Problems

"Where are my bogmallows?" yelled an unfriendly voice.

"Don't ask me," snapped another. "What did that Babysitter Fairy say? 'Picnics are scrummy?' Pah!"

Rachel gulped. There really *were* goblins nearby!

The shouting got louder and louder.

"No bogmallows anywhere? Terrible! *Terrible!*"

Kirsty leapt to her feet, her face pale with worry. The goblins were making such a din, they could only be lurking around the next bend.

"Me look?" trilled Tom, toddling after Kirsty.

Rachel scooped Tom up and stepped back towards the path. "We can't do anything while we're babysitting," she reminded her friend. "Let's take the twins to the picnic area. Mr and Mrs Robinson's lesson should be finished by now."

"It's that way," agreed Kirsty. "We'll get there faster if we give the twins a piggyback."

Lily and Tom giggled
and cheered as the
girls carried them
over stepping
stones, stooped
under vines and
waded through
swishy rushes.

"I can hear splashing," exclaimed
Rachel. "We must be getting close."

The trail curved one last time, then
opened out into a clearing in the
very heart of the dome. A stunning
waterfall tumbled over a tower of rocks,
little rainbows dancing in the spray.
All around the edge, tropical orchids
blossomed in hot shades of tangerine,
scarlet and pink. It was the perfect
location for a rainforest picnic.

"Mummy! Daddy!" cried Lily, wriggling down from Kirsty's back.

"Oh my," said Kirsty in a low voice. "What has happened here?"

The picnic area was in chaos. The Sunnydays team had put on a delicious spread, but half of the tables had collapsed, sending trays of sandwiches and cupcakes spilling to the ground.

Mrs Tate and Mrs Walker were laying out picnic rugs, but the blankets were splattered with mud. Diane was rushing around in a panic trying to find something for the hungry children to eat.

"It's a disaster!" she cried, rescuing a squashed plate of sausage rolls.

Kirsty squeezed Rachel's arm.

"Look at those sausage rolls," she whispered. "The pastry's turned green!"

Rachel gasped. Kirsty was right! Every sausage roll had a horrible green tinge to it, and so did the cakes.

"We've got to track down those goblins," Rachel urged. "They're spoiling the food!"

Kirsty and Rachel handed the twins back to Mrs Robinson, then ran off to find their parents.

"We had a great time on the lake," sighed Mr Tate, "but things have taken a turn for the worse!"

Mr Walker looked down at his shoe and groaned. "Now I've gone and stepped in jelly. How did that happen?"

"Do you mind if we head off for a while?" asked Rachel.

Mr Walker wiped the jelly off his shoe.

"You go, girls. We've got *plenty* to do here."

Within moments, Kirsty and Rachel were running back down the trail.

"Let's hide here," whispered Rachel, slipping behind a tree.

Kirsty peeped through the branches, then ducked back out of sight. Three grumpy goblins were sitting on tree stumps just a few metres away from them! The meanies were making a terrible racket.

"Give me that!" demanded one, swiping a teapot from his mate and swigging

from the spout.

"How rude!" snapped another, erupting into a giant goblin burp. "I bet those yucky fairy babies have enough drink and grub at their picnics!"

The third goblin sat with a messy tablecloth tied round his neck, rubbing his bloated belly.

"It's too hot in here," he groaned. "I feel icky…"

"You only feel sick cause you scoffed all the food," grumbled the burping goblin.

The first goblin put down his teapot and began to chuckle.

96

"At least we've spoilt Jennifer's fun," he guffawed. "She'll never guess where we've stashed her snack pack."

Kirsty and Rachel took a step closer and listened carefully.

"Hiding it in Fairyland was a brilliant idea," he continued. "It's right under their noses."

The poorly goblin wiped his mouth with the back of his hand.

"I've had enough of this," he announced. "Let's go back and fetch it. When we hand over the snack pack, Jack Frost is bound to give us a reward!"

Kirsty and Rachel froze on the spot, their eyes wide with worry. There was only one thing for it – they had to get to Fairyland first!

Off to Fairyland!

The goblins stomped out of the clearing, shoving and pushing each other through the bushes. As soon as the coast was clear, Kirsty and Rachel leapt out from their hiding spot.

"Poor Jennifer," sighed Kirsty. "We must warn her."

Rachel reached for her golden necklace and carefully opened the locket. Inside was a precious sprinkling of fairy dust.

"Let's hold hands," she suggested, as Kirsty opened her locket, too.

The best friends scattered a pinch of fairy dust into the air. A sweet-scented breeze instantly began to curl around their legs.

"Isn't it beautiful?" marvelled Kirsty, as the breeze transformed into a trail of exquisite rainbow colours. The enchanted rainbow swooshed around the girls, lifting them high into the air.

Kirsty and Rachel felt a tickle on their shoulders. A pair of shimmering fairy wings had

appeared on each girl's back! The girls
fluttered their wings and laughed – it was
wonderful to be fairies again.

After a while, the rainbow began to
arch back towards the ground. Kirsty
and Rachel found themselves floating
towards a wood dotted with blossom
trees. When their feet touched the grass,
the rainbow faded away as quickly as it
had arrived.

"Where are we?"
wondered Rachel,
breathing in the
country air. "I
don't think
we've visited
this part of
Fairyland
before."

Kirsty pointed to a toadstool cottage with jolly sunflowers growing in the garden. She fluttered up the path to the front door.

"Come here, Rachel!" she gasped, as soon as she got to the front door.

Above the bell, a hand-painted sign said in pink letters: JENNIFER — FAIRY BABYSITTER. The girls had discovered the Fairyland Nursery!

Kirsty stepped forward
and rang the bell. A
happy chime pealed
across the wood, but
no one answered.
She was just about
to turn away when
Rachel pointed to
a little path leading
around the cottage. "I

can hear voices," she whispered.

Kirsty and Rachel followed the path
round to the back of the cottage.

"How adorable!" gasped Rachel.
"Look!"

There, at the bottom of the garden,
was a circle of fairy babies. The gorgeous
creatures sat like cherubs, their delicate
gossamer wings twinkling in the sunlight.

103

The babies were dressed in romper
suits and little floppy sunhats. Each one
clutched a wand with a glowing star at
the very tip.

"Those must be training wands,"
guessed Kirsty.

"I can see Jennifer, too," added
Rachel.

The Babysitter Fairy was struggling
to open a picnic hamper packed full of
food. The girls fluttered up in the nick
of time. Just as they joined the circle, the
hamper fell face down onto the lawn!

"Oh dear," sighed Jennifer, watching as cupcakes, rolls and apples tumbled across the grass. "I should

have known this might happen!"

"We can help," offered Kirsty. Jennifer tried to greet her friends with a smile, but her sweet face was full of worry.

"Our picnic hasn't got off to a very good start," she confessed. "Without the magical snack pack, none of the food tastes nice."

Just then another fairy fluttered down
the path. Kirsty and Rachel recognised
the strawberry curls and shimmering blue
vest straight away – it
was Polly the Party
Fun Fairy!

"I'm here to
organise the
picnic party
games," Polly
explained, "but
they keep going
wrong! The donkey
for 'pin the tail on the
donkey' has cantered off and we've lost
the parcel to pass. Even the balloons
have gone flat."

"We overheard the goblins talking,"
announced Rachel. "The magical

snack pack is in Fairyland…and they're coming to get it!"

"We must find it first," replied Jennifer. "If Jack Frost steals the snack pack, all mealtimes will be ruined!

"I'll babysit while you search," Polly offered kindly.

"Where shall we start?" asked Rachel, darting up towards the cottage as fast as her wings could carry her.

Kirsty thought hard. The goblin had said that he'd hidden the snack pack right under the fairies' noses. What did he mean?

Suddenly her face lit up.

"Jennifer," she said. "Can you show us inside the Fairyland Nursery? I think the goblins have played a trick on us."

Lost then Found

"This way!" cried Jennifer.

Kirsty and Rachel followed the Babysitter Fairy through a quaint red kitchen, up a twisting set of stairs and out into the Nursery playroom.

"It's just as magical as I knew it would be," exclaimed Rachel, remembering the pictures Jennifer had revealed in the Seeing Pool only a day before.

109

Kirsty flitted past the row of tiny cots and sweet fairy teddy bears.

"That goblin hid the snack pack where a fairy would never think of looking," she remarked. "Where do you keep your magical objects, Jennifer?"

Jennifer pointed to a bookshelf tucked away in the farthest corner of the playroom. Three quilted cushions were neatly lined up along the top shelf. The first one had the magical toy box on top.

"Look underneath the middle one," urged Rachel.

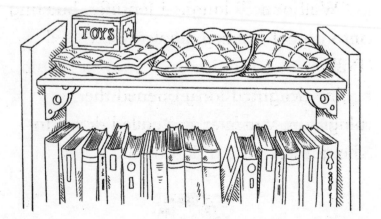

Jennifer darted up
to the top shelf
and lifted up
the cushion.
Suddenly her
wand began to
fizz with scarlet
stars!

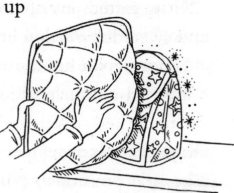

"It's here!" she cried,
pulling out the magical snack pack.

Rachel and Kirsty beamed at each
other. Trust the silly goblins to hide their
booty in the place where it belonged!

"Well done," laughed Jennifer, bursting
into a peal of fairy giggles. "Let's tell
Polly."

The delighted fairy opened the
playroom window and called down to
the garden.

"Now picnics everywhere can be fun again," added Rachel, thinking of Lily and Tom in the rainforest dome.

"Not if I can help it!" bellowed a voice.

Kirsty and Rachel shivered in surprise as bony green fingers plucked the snack pack out of Jennifer's hands.

"It's the goblin from the picnic!" cried Kirsty.

The greedy goblin smirked. The mischievous creature had climbed in through the toadstool window.

"That's me!" he boasted. "This snack pack is going to live in Jack Frost's Ice Castle."

"No," sobbed Jennifer. "Please give it back!"

The goblin guffawed loudly.

"We've got to do something," said Kirsty breathlessly.

Rachel fluttered up to the ceiling. She circled round and round the playroom, leaving a trail of fairy dust shimmering in the air behind her. The goblin stumbled and shouted, swiping at her with his free hand.

"Stop it!" he groaned. "You're making me dizzy!"

"Faster," urged Kirsty, her eyes twinkling with delight.

Rachel looped again and again. The angry goblin lunged at her but missed, blundering into a fairy cot instead. When he got back to his feet, there was a dainty lace curtain caught on his sticky-out ears.

Kirsty spotted her chance.

"Give us back the snack pack now," she demanded.

"Shan't!" pouted the goblin. "I want a reward from Jack Frost."

Jennifer bravely stepped a little closer. "I've got an even better reward," she said. "How would you like a stinky goblin picnic full of yucky foods?"

114

"You wouldn't have to share," added Kirsty.

"That's right!" piped up Rachel. "Smelly cauliflower, rotten eggs and a pile of bogmallows. It's all yours."

The greedy creature paused for a moment to lick his lips.

"Nah," he decided. "I don't trust you fairies!"

With that the intruder tucked the magical snack pack under his arm and flung open the playroom door.

"Goblin!"

The thief howled in panic. A gorgeous group of fairy babies were fluttering up the stairs!

The little tots gurgled at the sight of the funny-looking stranger. Some even held their arms out for a cuddle.

"Don't you like fairy babies?" Rachel asked innocently.

The goblin shuffled nervously from foot to foot.

"They're just as cute as human ones," chimed Kirsty.

"Horrible things, all of them," he yowled, pressing the magical snack pack into Jennifer's hands. "Keep your precious object. I'm off!"

Bang!

The goblin marched out of the playroom, slamming the door behind him.

The fairies were delighted. Jennifer held her arms out, wrapping each of the dear

little tots in
a hug.

"Let's start
the picnic all
over again,"
she beamed.
"Kirsty,
Rachel, will
you join us?"

The best friends
shared a secret smile.

"Not this time," replied Kirsty. "Two
very special babies are waiting for us in
the human world."

"That's right," Rachel agreed. "We
can't be late for the rainforest picnic!"

The Stolen Nightlight

Contents

Lanterns by the Lake

"What good sticking, Tom," said Kirsty with a smile. "Clever boy!"

Rachel crouched down to admire Lily's handiwork.

"Look!" she exclaimed. "Lily's nearly ready to start painting."

It was Kirsty and Rachel's last full day at EcoWorld, and the friends were keen to make the most of every minute.

After breakfast they'd brought the twins down to the lake for a make-and-do morning. Diane from the Sunnydays Kids' Club was running an outdoor craft session.

"This really is a perfect spot, isn't it?" Rachel sighed happily.

"Bliss!" agreed Kirsty. "And making recycled paper lanterns is such a lovely idea."

The man-made lake was set in the middle of an airy dome, fitted with a special roof that could be pulled back on dry days like today. Diane had set up a row of tables along the lake's sandy beach. A dozen happy little children sat clutching glue sticks, crayons, glitter and tape.

"Ra-ra!" squealed Lily, finding a

124

paintbrush and pointing to the pink
paint. "You do it?"

"Let's decorate it together," suggested
Rachel. "What would you like to paint
on your lantern?"

Sweet little dimples suddenly appeared
in Lily's cheeks.

"Fairies!" she squealed. "Lily like
fairies!"

"I like fairies, too," smiled Rachel,
catching Kirsty's eye.

With her golden curls and polka-dot pinafore dress, Lily reminded the friends of the adorable fairy babies in Jennifer the Babysitter Fairy's nursery. All she needed was a star-topped training wand and a tiny pair of fairy wings!

While Rachel and Lily got painting, Kirsty helped Tom tape up the sides of his lantern. "We'll come back to the lake later and watch them fly high into the air," she explained.

"Higher than me?" wondered Tom, his eyes open wide.

Kirsty laughed. "Yes, much higher than you!"

Diane wandered up to see how the children were getting on.

"The roof is going to stay open this evening," she said. "The lanterns will float right up to the sky! There's going to be a barbecue and songs around the campfire."

Tom and Lily beamed at each other. It sounded magical!

"I just hope that Jack Frost doesn't spoil their fun," Rachel murmured under her breath. "Jennifer is still missing one magical object."

Kirsty frowned. Without the Babysitter Fairy's nightlight, children's sleep times were sure to go terribly wrong.

"Let's take the twins for a walk around the park," she suggested. "We might spot a clue."

"Good idea!" replied Rachel.

The girls wrote the twins' names on their lanterns, then laid them out to dry. After letting Diane know where they were going, they wandered down the boardwalk that led out to the main park.

128

"Where do we start?" wondered
Rachel.

She squinted up
at a wooden
post with signs
pointing in
every direction.
Should they try
the rainforest
dome, the
Treetop Café or
the eco-centre?

Just then, a hoot of
laughter echoed through the trees.

"Hurry up!" yelled a voice.

"Stop pushing!" shouted another. "I'm
getting in there first!"

Rachel reached for Tom and Lily's
hands.

The din got louder and louder. Kirsty had heard that sort of racket before... from goblins!

The best friends felt their hearts thump as the bushes began to rustle and shake. Three shadowy figures burst through the trees. The rowdy group were all dressed in wetsuits reaching all the way down to the ankle. Kirsty and Rachel peered at the strangers' feet, searching for a glimpse of green.

"This way!" yelled a lad with blond hair, pointing to a sign saying SPLASH PARK.

"Awesome!" cheered his friend, shoving to the front.

Rachel sighed. These weren't goblins at all! It was just a bunch of boys on their way to the swimming centre.

"Where now?" asked Kirsty, putting her hands on her hips. "It's not long until Tom and Lily's nap. We can't let Jack Frost spoil their last day at EcoWorld!"

Nap Nuisance

"The twins are starting to look sleepy," said Rachel, leading Tom and Lily back onto the path.

"Want Mummy," sighed Tom, holding out his arms to be carried. Lily trailed behind her brother, sucking her thumb.

"Let's take them back to the lodge," suggested Kirsty. "We might find something on the way."

"Would you like another piggyback ride?" asked Rachel.

Tom nodded sleepily.

The girls lifted the twins onto their backs, then slowly made their way along the trail.

"Hello, girls!" grinned Mr Tate, as the friends finally trooped through the gate at the bottom of the garden. "You're just in time for lunch."

Mr and Mrs Walker looked up from their sunloungers and waved. Mrs Tate placed a big bowl of pasta in the middle of the garden table.

"Thank you for taking Tom and Lily out." Mrs Robinson smiled, putting down her magazine.

"I'd better get the twins into their cots straight away," she said. "We want them to have lots of energy for the campfire and barbecue tonight!"

"Can we help?" asked Rachel, running in to find Lily's favourite rag doll.

Mrs Robinson nodded. "That would be lovely, thank you."

Kirsty and Rachel carried Tom and Lily into their bedroom. Mrs Robinson pulled the curtains, while the girls clipped the twins into their fleecy sleeping bags. It was a lovely room for a nap – baby rabbits scampered and hopped along the wallpaper and rainbow mobiles spun gently from the ceiling.

"Night night," whispered Rachel.

"No, Ra-ra!" squealed Lily, sitting up again.

Rachel tried to lay the little girl back down, but she clenched her fists and refused. At the same time, Tom reached for the cot bars and pulled himself up.

"No sleeps!" he called, bouncing up and down on the mattress.

"This isn't like them," worried Mrs Robinson, searching for the twins' nightlight. "They usually love their lunchtime nap."

d to comfort Lily, but the

her head and threw her

onto the carpet. Tom clung on to the cot bars and began to cry.

Mrs Robinson rummaged through the twin's cupboards.

"Where has that nightlight gone?" she asked out loud. "Lily and Tom love the lullabies it plays."

The twins began to sob even more loudly. Mrs Robinson was relieved when Mr Robinson stuck his head round the door to find out what all the fuss was about.

"We'll leave you to settle the twins," suggested Rachel, sharing a knowing look with Kirsty.

The friends rushed out to the garden so they could talk properly.

"The twins won't settle until Jennifer's magical nightlight is back where it belongs," sighed Kirsty. "We've got to keep looking!"

The girls checked with their parents,
then hurried out to the park. As they ran
along the trail, they could hear babies
crying in the other eco-lodges.

"She can't nap without her nightlight!"
they heard one frazzled mum call.

"He won't even shut
his eyes," insisted
another dad,
pacing up
and down
his garden
with a
baby in a
sling.

"This is
serious," said
Rachel urgently.

"None of the children can get to sleep!"

"Let's head back to the forest," suggested Kirsty.

She climbed over a stile, then darted into a pretty tunnel of willow trees. The branches seemed to bend and curve towards them, hiding the girls from view.

"Look behind you," whispered Rachel.

Kirsty spun round. Somehow, the branches had closed over the entrance to the path! The girls found themselves standing in a secret den covered in fluttering green leaves.

"My fingers are tingling!" gasped Kirsty.

"Oh, Kirsty," marvelled Rachel. "We're being called to Fairyland!"

Trouble at Twilight

A burst of glittering light swooshed around Kirsty and Rachel, twirling the girls round and round. The willow branches began to sway, their leaves shimmering in green and gold.

Kirsty felt her toes lift off the path. "We're shrinking to fairy-size!" she cried.

Rachel smiled, then reached for her best friend's hand.

At that moment, a delicate pair of

gossamer wings appeared on each girl's shoulders. The willow trees parted again, and the girls fluttered out into the warm afternoon sunlight.

A moment later, the girls were standing in a country garden dotted with beautiful golden sunflowers. A long curved path led up to an enchanting toadstool cottage.

"It's the Fairyland Nursery!" exclaimed Kirsty.

A fairy with curly black hair opened a window

and peeped outside.

"I'm so thrilled to see you again!" she called. "Do come in."

When Rachel and Kirsty got to the back door, they recognised Sabrina the Sweet Dreams Fairy. The friends shared a warm hug – remembering the time they helped Sabrina and the Twilight Fairies get their bags of magical dust back from Jack Frost.

"Follow me, girls," Sabrina said hastily.

"Jennifer needs your help."

Rachel and Kirsty fluttered down
the hallway as quickly as they could.
When they got to the playroom, they
couldn't believe their eyes. There were
fairy babies clambering up the canopies,
hiding in toy boxes and crawling under
cupboards. The other Twilight Fairies
were rushing up and down trying to
coax the little ones back into their cots.
Even Yasmin the Night Owl Fairy's

magical bag of sleep dust didn't seem to be working. Poor Jennifer stood in the middle of the chaos clutching a pile of pillows.

Pouf!

Suddenly the pillows that Jennifer had been carrying changed into a stack of silly dressing-up clothes. A little fairy in a stripy sleepsuit had crawled up and touched it with her star-topped wand!

"Please *try* and remember the rules,

Ellie," sighed Jennifer, placing the funny hats and frilly frocks onto a chair. "No magic at naptime."

The cheeky baby peeped up at the Babysitter Fairy then burst into a peal of fairy giggles. It was impossible to be cross with the tot, but poor Jennifer's face looked tired and sad.

"If fairy babies miss their sleep, their spells start going haywire," she explained. "When Morgan popped in to help this afternoon, a stray bolt of baby magic turned her hair blue! It will take hours to fade back to normal again."

Morgan the Midnight Fairy peeped her head out from underneath a nearby cot. The fairy's lovely blonde hair really had turned as blue as her dress!

Rachel squeezed Jennifer's hand. "What can we do to help?" she asked.

"We have to get my nightlight back before bedtime," replied the flustered fairy. "Missing a nap is one thing, but who knows what will happen if none of the babies sleep tonight!"

Kirsty thought for a moment. "If the nightlight isn't in Fairyland or the human world, then there's only one place left to try," she announced. "Jack Frost's Ice Castle!"

Into the Ice Castle

"Hold on tight, everyone!" called Jennifer. "Please try and stay in line."

Kirsty and Rachel shared a secret smile. It was hard to believe that they were fluttering through the sky hand in hand with a dozen adorable fairy babies! When the friends had decided to go to the Ice Castle, Jennifer thought it best to bring the little ones along, too, so she could look after them. The Twilight

Fairies couldn't babysit any longer, as they had to get ready for their night's work.

"Don't let go of my hand," Kirsty whispered gently into the ear of a tiny tot with dancing green eyes.

The toddler flipped onto her tummy, then burst into cheeky chuckles.

Although fairy babies could fly, they couldn't resist zooming off in zigzags or dizzy loop-the-loops. Jennifer had insisted that all the babies fly in a row so that no one got separated. Kirsty was posted at one end of the flying crocodile line and Rachel at the other. The Babysitter Fairy flew in the middle of the line, so she could keep an eye on everyone.

Suddenly, way off in the distance, they could see the spiky silhouette of Jack Frost's Ice Castle. As the fairies got closer, the air turned cold. Soon they were fluttering round the castle's icy turrets.

"Let's slip in here," suggested Rachel, pointing to a narrow window.

Jennifer waved her wand and whispered a spell, making the fairies so small that they could slip into the castle unseen.

She shushed the fairy babies, who thought being silent was a wonderful new game.

The group fluttered through the castle's gloomy corridors without making a sound. Rachel took the lead, darting left and right as they fluttered past dungeons, kitchens and frozen staircases. There wasn't a goblin in sight.

"Here's the Throne Room," breathed Kirsty, approaching an enormous pair of wrought-iron doors.

Jennifer called all the fairy babies around her and asked them to listen carefully.

"Everyone fly up near the ceiling, please," she said.

155

"It's important to stay out of sight."

The fairies darted into the Throne Room through a tiny gap in the door. Hordes of goblins were lying on the stone floor, dressed in nightshirts or pyjamas. Each had a little nightlight beside them, but not a single creature was sleeping. Instead they were throwing blankets around, poking out their tongues and splurting hot chocolate everywhere!

"This way, fairies," whispered Kirsty, pointing up to the ceiling. "Hide up there!"

The fairy babies fluttered up to the crystal chandelier in the centre of the Throne Room, their little eyes full of wonder.

"What was that?" barked a goblin, feeling a tiny breeze rush past his nose.

"Don't ask me!" bellowed his friend, whacking another goblin round the head with a pillow. "Take this instead!"

157

The goblin next to him tried to get up and fight back, but his big green feet were caught up in his sleeping bag. The silly creature landed on his mates with a noisy bump, sending nightlights scattering in all directions.

Up on the chandelier, the fairy babies collapsed into delighted giggles. They thought it was the funniest thing they'd ever seen!

"Those nightlights have been stolen from the human world," Rachel told Kirsty.

"My magical nightlight's here, too," whispered Jennifer. "Look!"

The Babysitter Fairy pointed at Jack Frost's ice-blue throne, sitting in the centre of the room. The Ice Lord himself was slumped in the seat, holding the magical nightlight! But he looked thoroughly miserable.

"Why won't this thing work?" he grumbled, giving the nightlight a hard shake. "Stupid fairy magic!"

159

The friends flew as close to Jack Frost
as they dared. As soon as Jennifer set
her tiny feet on the top of his throne,
the magical nightlight began to glow. A
sweet lullaby
started to
play. Jack
Frost leapt
to his feet in
surprise!

"What are
you doing
here?" he
thundered as
he spotted
the fairies.

"I'm here
for the nightlight," Jennifer piped up
boldly. "It belongs to me."

Jack Frost snatched up the magical nightlight, then dangled it over the side of the throne with one bony finger. The fairy babies on the chandelier shrieked in surprise.

"It's useless!" he snapped. "I thought your silly objects would help make my goblins behave, but none of them worked. I'm going to smash it up!"

Bedtime at Last

"The nightlight only works for true babysitters," explained Jennifer. "You must want the children in your care to be safe and happy, *not* obey your every command!"

"Pah!" barked Jack Frost, turning his back in a sulk.

Kirsty and Rachel spotted their chance. The friends darted forwards and Rachel grabbed the nightlight.

"Jennifer!" called Rachel, tossing the enchanted object through the air. "Catch!"

As soon as it landed in the Babysitter Fairy's arms the magical nightlight began to glow even more brightly, casting shapes across the Throne Room walls.

Jack Frost's face turned white with rage. He swiped at Jennifer but missed, landing in a furious heap.

"Goblins!" he screeched. "Get those pesky fairies!"

Kirsty nudged Rachel in the ribs. "Jack Frost's goblins aren't listening!"

Now the magical nightlight was working again, the fairy babies had fluttered down from the chandelier. The dear little things were trying to snuggle up on the blankets beside the goblins!

Instead of grabbing the fairies, Jack
Frost's henchmen were wailing pitifully
and scrambling to get away.

"Ugh!" shuddered
one. "This one's
trying to
cuddle me.
Get it off!"

"Help!"
yelled
another,
trying to shake
an adorable fairy
toddler off his sleeping bag.

"Of course!" grinned Rachel. "Goblins
can't bear babies – human or fairy
ones!"

"Luckily babies *love* goblins!" replied
Kirsty.

A terrified goblin glanced up at the pretty shadows the nightlight was flicking across the castle walls.

"It gets worse!" he shouted, pointing at the silhouettes. "Now giant pogwurzels are coming to get us!"

The room dissolved into shrieking as panicked goblins fled in every direction. Jack Frost sat in the middle with his face in his hands.

"It's nearly fairy bedtime," said Jennifer. "Shall we go home?"

167

Once the fairy babies were all settled in
their cots back at the Fairyland Nursery,
Jennifer sat down to read them a bedtime
story.

"Why don't we have
*Spikilocks and the
Three Goblins*,"
suggested the
Babysitter Fairy,
touching an old
leather-covered
book with her wand.

Kirsty and Rachel
watched spellbound as a parade of tiny
storybook characters tripped through the
air above the babies' heads. The story
was so enchanting, even they couldn't
help feeling a little sad when Jennifer
closed the book and said it was the end.

168

"Sweet dreams," smiled Kirsty, fluttering from cot to cot.

"It was magical meeting you," added Rachel, kissing each of the babies goodnight.

Jennifer turned on her nightlight, filling the room with a warm glow. A lovely lullaby began to play.

"I can't thank you enough," she whispered, wrapping the girls in a tight hug. "Now little ones everywhere can be happy and safe again!"

"And we've got some babysitting to do tonight," said Kirsty. "Haven't we, Rachel?"

Rachel thought of Lily and Tom. The friends couldn't miss their last night in the lodge!

"Right, then just close your eyes," said Jennifer. "Goodbye, girls!"

Kirsty and Rachel held hands and shut their eyes tight. When they opened them again, they were back to normal size and standing by the side of the lake in EcoWorld. A stunning silver moon shone down on the water, a thousand tiny stars twinkling brightly behind it.

"Lantern time!" cried Tom, wrapping his arms around Kirsty's legs, as the girls wandered up to the Tates, Walkers and Robinsons.

Lily squealed with pleasure. "Ra-ra!" she grinned, holding out her paper lantern.

Rachel gasped. The lanterns had been transformed. Each one sparkled in the moonlight, glinting with tiny gemstones and pearls.

"It must be fairy magic," whispered Kirsty to Rachel, as she lifted Tom into the air.

Mrs Robinson came over to the girls. "Enjoy the magical sight!" She smiled. "Afterwards we'll pop the little ones to bed."

Rachel beamed at Kirsty. She had a feeling that the twins were going to sleep well tonight!

Now it's time for Kirsty and Rachel to help...

Lottie the Lollipop Fairy

Read on for a sneak peek...

"I can't *wait* for you to meet my aunt Harri, Rachel!" Kirsty Tate exclaimed, beaming at her best friend, Rachel Walker. Rachel had arrived that morning to spend the spring half-term holiday with Kirsty in the pretty village of Wetherbury. "Mum's invited her to come to lunch today, so you'll be able to ask Aunt Harri all about *Candy Land*."

Rachel grinned. "I can't wait to meet Aunt Harri, either," she replied. "Working in a sweet factory must be one of the most wonderful jobs in the whole world!"

"I guess it's *almost* as wonderful as being a fairy," Kirsty said, and the girls shared a secret smile. They'd had many thrilling adventures with their fairy friends and hoped to have many more.

"The *Candy Land* factory is on a hill overlooking Wetherbury," Kirsty explained. "Aunt Harri gets lots of free sweets and she always brings a big bagful with her whenever she comes to visit."

"Oh, I'm looking forward to meeting her even more, then!" Rachel laughed.

There was a ring at the doorbell and the girls rushed to answer it. Outside stood a smiling, fair-haired young woman holding a bulging pink-and-white striped carrier bag. *Candy Land* was written across the side of the bag in sparkly silver glitter.

"Hello, Kirsty," Aunt Harri said,

giving her a big hug. "And you must be
Rachel." She hugged Rachel, too. "I've
heard so much about you from Kirsty."

"I've heard lots about you, too,"
Rachel replied, smiling back.

"Then I'm sure Kirsty's told you all
about *Candy Land*!" Aunt Harri said,
her big blue eyes twinkling. "I thought
you might like to try some of our
sweets." And she handed the bag to the
girls.

Eagerly, Rachel and Kirsty peeked
inside. They could see lollipops,
chocolate bars, and piles of other sweets
wrapped in shiny coloured paper.
However, to their dismay, the sweets
looked broken and battered and not
at all appetising. But, most unexpected
of all, there was a horrible smell inside
the bag that made both girls gasp and

draw back slightly. What on earth was that smell, Rachel thought, trying not to wrinkle up her nose in disgust. The sweets looked and smelt like rotting rubbish! But she didn't want to be rude and complain when Aunt Harri had been kind enough to bring them the sweets. Kirsty, too, was trying to smile politely at her aunt.

"Maybe we should wait until after lunch to try them," Kirsty suggested, closing the bag quickly.

Aunt Harri's face fell. "The sweets are really bad, aren't they?" she sighed. "Girls, something's gone terribly wrong at *Candy Land*. All the sweets look, smell and taste absolutely horrid!"

Read **Lottie the Lollipop Fairy** to find out what adventures are in store for Kirsty and Rachel!

Competition!

Jennifer the Babysitter Fairy has created this
special word wand just for you!
Read the clues and write the answers in the boxes.
The last letter of each word is the start of the next one.
When you have all three answers, go online to enter.

Which one of Jennifer's magical objects helps children sleep peacefully?

☆ ☆ ☆ ☆ ☆ ☆ ☆ ☆ ☆ ☆ ☆

What is Kirsty's surname?

☆ ☆ ☆ ☆ ☆

What is the name of the holiday camp that Kirsty and Rachel go to?

☆ ☆ ☆ ☆ ☆ ☆ ☆ ☆ ☆ ☆

We will put all the correct entries into a draw and select a winner to
receive a special Rainbow Magic Goodie Bag featuring lots of treats
for you and your fairy friends.

You'll also star in a new Rainbow Magic story!

Enter online now at www.rainbowmagicbooks.co.uk